T0198890

# Alexander Anthony Finds A Great Love

By Anthony Mayfield

Illustrations by Samuka (Larry Cook)

This is a work of fiction. Names, characters,
places and incidents either are the product of the
author's imagination or are used fictitiously, and any
resemblance to any actual persons, living or dead,
events, or locales is entirely coincidental.

To order additional copies of this book, contact:
Xlibris
844-714-8691
www.Xlibris.com
Orders@Xlibris.com

ISBN:   Softcover        978-1-4134-3778-2
        Hardcover        978-1-4134-4168-0
        EBook            978-1-4771-8141-6

Print information available on the last page

Rev. date: 05/24/2022

By Anthony C. Mayfield

Illustrated by Larry Cook

Dedicated to God, Family, Friends and Children


May the world learn peace, love and laughter through its children.

"The clouds must be on vacation," Alexander Anthony thought, as he gazed into a spotless sky. And, while the sun was out, it wasn't hot. Well, it wasn't hot to Alexander. Nonetheless, the grownups complained about it being "Oh, so hot." But to Alexander, it was a beautiful day.

Alexander was eight years old. He had curly black hair and smooth pecan colored skin and, when standing erect, he stood exactly three feet, eight inches tall. Tired of hearing the adults talk about the weather, he decided to go outside. He stood in the doorway and let the light from the sun bathe his eyes while a gentle breeze tussled with the locks of his hair. "Ah, it's a beautiful day. It's not too hot," he said.

Looking out over his large backyard and wondering what he should do, a thought crossed his mind. He dashed back into the house. Minutes later, he emerged wearing his royal blue cape and the fancy paper crown that his grandfather had skillfully made especially for him. He was now the official king of the backyard. Walking triumphantly around the yard with his cape flapping behind him, he noticed a small, round mound. He ran up the side of the mound, leaped on top of it and proclaimed himself king and sole ruler of the backyard.

Unknown to Alexander, his grandfather was tired of talking about the weather too. He had gone into the kitchen to get himself a tall glass of lemonade. While he was in the kitchen, he peered out the window and watched as Alexander paraded around the yard with splendor and pomp making loud annunciations.

Sidetracked for a moment, Alexander noticed a group of ants busily at work. Without notice, a few of the ants crawled onto Alexander's leg and began biting him.

"Ouch!" He yelled. He knocked the ants off of his leg. And, because a few of the ants had bit him, he began to squash and stomp on all of the ants in sight until there were no more ants to be found. Then, remembering what his mother had told him after he'd been disciplined, he said, "I did it because I love you." Then he laughed out loud. He perched himself back on top of the mound, and with both hands on his hips he bellowed once again, "I am the king."

Having seen and heard Alexander, Grandpa went to the back door and called for him, "Alexander."

"Yes Grandpa," Alexander answered.

"Come here, I want to talk to you." Alexander started running back to the porch with his cape flapping in the wind behind him. "Look Grandpa, I'm flying."

"Yes, I know you are. Now fly on up here," Grandpa said.

"What is it Grandpa?" Alexander inquisitively asked. "Do you have some money, or maybe some candy, or a toy for me?"

"No, none of that. I do have something for you though."

"If it's not important stuff like money, candy, or toys, then what is it Gramps?"

"Well, it's much more important than all of those things; it's the greatest gift of all. It's God's love."

"God's love? What makes that so great and where is it?" Alexander asked.

"Well, Grandpa began, I saw what you did to those ants and afterwards you said that you did it because you loved them. Actually, you were being mean to them but you did make a point."

"I did, what point?"

"Well, you showed that love sometimes has to be tough, but when love is tough, it's always, always for good reasons. And the best-est love of all is God's love; it's warm and ticklish. It makes you smile and feel real good inside and out. It's better than ice cream and cake, and it's more fun than going to a carnival. And I'm going to give it to you."

"Where is it Gramps? I want it."

"Here it is, right here in the palm of my hands."

"Where Grandpa, I don't see anything."

"Well, it's there. When you first receive it you can't always see it and you don't always feel it, but it's real and it's there. As you get used to it, you will be able to spot it right away. What seems invisible to you now, will soon be crystal clear. The best thing about God's Love is that it's great: greater than anything and anybody, especially when it's in the heart of man. And now it's yours." Then Grandpa took his hand and pushed the Love of God right into Alexander's heart.

"That's it?" Alexander asked with a puzzled look on his face.

"Yes, that's it," Grandpa answered.

"Well, I don't feel anything. I don't even feel any different."

"That's quite all right, Grandpa said. Remember, you don't have to try real hard to see it or to feel it. Just get acquainted with it first and, by and by, you will see it in just about everything. In fact, when you aren't really paying attention, or when you least expect it, that's when you will see or feel it the most. Ok, I've given you the best love in the world, which is all that you need to be happy and successful. That's all that I've got. You can go play now."

"But what if I lose it before I see it, or what if the wind blows it away, what then Grandpa?"

"Well, if that should happen, just reach right into the air and pull yourself some more of God's Love out. But remember, you have got to get it in your heart in a hurry so that you will be able to see it. Then if you take it out, at least you will be able to spot it."

"Ok", Grandpa said again, "you can go now."

Slowly Alexander eased down and walked back to the yard. On the way, he pulled the Love of God out of his heart. He sniffed it but couldn't smell anything. He licked it, but it had no taste. He shook it but it didn't make a sound. "Hmp, this isn't so great," he said. He eased the love back into his heart, took his hat and cape off, and went and sat under the big old shade tree to ponder about, and to further examine his gift of love. After thinking about it for a minute, he decided to put God's Love to the test. He was certain that Grandpa, for the first time, had made an awful mistake. He was equally certain that there was something greater than God's Love, there just had to be, and he was going to find it and prove to himself and to Grandpa that God's Love wasn't so great.

He ran around to the side of the house and crawled into the giant refrigerator box that his mom let him have. It had written in capital letters the words "IMAGINA-TION EXPLORATION." He sat down on an old foam cushion that served as his pilot's chair, pushed some imaginary buttons, closed his eyes, and instantly, in his mind's eye, he was whisked away. When he opened his eyes, he found himself in the middle of a vast, Redwood forest.

He leaned back and looked up, but he could barely see any sky at all. The Redwood trees blocked almost all of the sunlight, and appeared to grow right into the sky. Alexander walked around until he found a Redwood tree that had been toppled by a lightening bolt. He looked down into the massive hole left by the uprooted Redwood. The hole seemed bottomless and it went straight to the belly of the earth.

Alexander pulled the Love of God out of his heart and when he did, this time he felt a twinge of emptiness. He clutched the love and, looking into the hole, he thought about how great the earth is; "after all," he reasoned, "if the earth holds all of the deserts, all of the forests, and even the mightiest of mountains, surely it will be able to hold the Love of God, which would make it greater than the Love of God." With that, he leaned over the hole, opened his hand, and dropped the love into the belly of the earth.

He could hear the love tumble end over end and bounce off of the sides of the hole until it hit the bottom with a faint splash far, far below. For the longest moment, it seemed like nothing was happening or was going to happen. Alexander leaned further over the hole and strained to hear something... actually, any sound at all would have made him think that something was happening but all that he heard was a deafening silence. Since nothing to his satisfaction happened, he stood, looked down in the hole one more time and said, "Hmp, some great love." When he turned to walk away, a strange belching sound came from the bottom of the hole followed by a heady gust of wind.

Alexander turned and looked back down into the hole: nothing. When he turned back around to walk away, to his amazement, every kind of tree, flower, bush, and all that the earth grew, had sprung up or was growing right before his eyes in the most radiant of colors all over the face of the earth!

Then, without warning, a moan erupted from the belly of the earth. The ground began to shake violently, the Redwood trees shook, mountains shook, buildings shook, and everything on, and in the earth was terribly shaken. Then, the earth cracked open and spew out the love that Alexander had dropped into it.

Out of the cracked and steaming ground, a voice spoke and said, "I couldn't hold the Love of God then, and I can't hold it now; it's just too great, great, great..." said the earth in an echoing, low voice.

"Wow, that's incredible," Alexander said, as he picked up the Love of God and slipped it back into his heart. "Maybe," he thought, "the earth is just too small to hold the Love of God. I know! There's more water than there is land, surely the sea can hold this love. After all, the sea holds icebergs, submarines, whales, and sunken treasures; hmp, why the sea even holds the earth, so I know it can hold the Love of God."

With that, he ran back to his Explorer Transporter and, once inside, he pushed the imaginary buttons, pulled some imaginary knobs, closed his eyes and zoomed away in the comfort and luxury of his fertile mind.

This time, when he opened his eyes he was standing on an isolated, white sandy beach. High above him, sea gulls were gliding effortlessly on puffs of wind while fish snapped at insects that droned too close to the waters edge in a tiny cove down the beach. Overblown, picturesque clouds formed an idyllic background as they floated lazily across the sky.

Just up the beach, no more than twenty yards away from where Alexander had landed, a canoe was tied to a makeshift pier that jut awkwardly out into the sea. Alexander ran over to the little boat, untied it and jumped in. He grabbed the oars that were-lying in the bottom of the boat and began to row out towards the middle of the sea. It took all of his strength to maneuver the canoe because, like little boys on playgrounds, the sea was rough and tumble. Even so, after many long hours had elapsed, Alexander, sore, sweaty, and tired had made it to the very middle of the sea. He sat motionless for a moment so that he could catch his breath. The little boat was bobbing like a cork as the water slapped and wrestled with its sides.

Alexander pulled the Love of God from his pounding heart and dropped it into the gurgling, hungry sea. "Plup," was the sound the love made when it came in contact with the water. He could see that a little whirlpool had formed on the spot where the love had gone in. Again, for the longest time, it seemed like nothing was happening or was going to happen. Then, just as Alexander was about to give up on God for the second time, the sea suddenly got quiet. Waves reared up, arched, stretched out, and then lay flat as the sea turned from a murky green to a clear blue.

And the waters were blue beyond the middle of the sea, beyond as far as the eye could see, and all the way to where the waters touched the ends of the earth, there was nothing but crystal clear, blue waters that danced and tickled the earth's shores all over the world.

Following the quiet serenity, the sea began to foam and bubble, as if it were boiling. Suddenly, waves rose up again, this time like angry fists, and began to smite each other while the sea swelled, raged, and rocked back and forth. Then, a mighty tidal wave grew underneath Alexander's fragile little boat and lifted him and the boat high into the air and rushed hastily towards the distant shore. It ran right up to the beach and gently placed the canoe on the sandy shore.

Alexander stood in the boat and watched as the foam receded. From his advantage point, he could see sharks, whales, fish, eels, octopus, and all the living creatures of all the seas everywhere. They swam close to the edge of the water and, one by one, to Alexander's surprise, they spat a piece of the Love of God out onto the shore. After each one had given up its piece, the pieces came together to form the one initial piece. And from miles and miles away, over the deep rumble of the sea, Alexander listened as the gurgling voice of the sea spoke.

"The last time I felt this love inside of me, it caused me to part right down the middle. So, this time, rather than being divided again, each living creature within me quickly attacked and devoured as much of the Love of God as it could hold. Since the love didn't appear to be that big, I thought that it could easily be consumed by a small school of minnow. But, even after they had eaten to the point of being bloated, there was still some left. So I sent a larger school of fish and they ate until they, too, were full. And on and on went the process until every living creature that lives within water had consumed as much of the Love of God as possible and yet there was still some left over. Alas, this love, His Love, is just too great. So, we are returning it from whence it came." With that, the tidal wave and all of the creatures of the sea withdrew and vanished quietly behind the veil that separates all that man knows about the sea from what he does not know and everything returned to normal.

Alexander picked up the love, smiled, and slipped it back into his heart. He was about to get back into the Explorer when he heard an airborne Sea Gull cry out to his mate. "Hmm," Alexander thought, "the sky is greater than both land and sea combined. It's so great that no man can see all of it at one time. I know," he said excitedly, "I'll shoot the Love of God into the sky; surely, if the sky can hold clouds, stars, the sun, and the moon, it will be able to hold the Love of God.

Once again, he used his vivid imagination, closed his eyes, and thought of what he would need to get the love deep into the sky. When he opened his eyes, there on the floor of the Explorer was a huge bow and arrow and a coil of thin, unbreakable twine. He tied one end of the twine to the Love of God and the other end to the arrow and, placing the arrow inside of the bow, he pulled back with all of his might, aimed for the center of the sky, and let it fling. The arrow streaked through the sky and disappeared behind a group of clouds.

Alexander shielded his eyes from the sun and tried to locate the arrow. He looked until his neck became stiff and until his eyes burned from the fiery, bright sun. Disappointed, he went and plopped himself down on a big rock that protruded into the sea. Racing waves dashed in and crashed noisily against the rock leaving a bed of foam that made a "*shooshing*" sound as the waves went back out to race in again.

Occasionally, he would rare back and look into the sky to see if anything was happening but whenever he did, a stiff pain would rise up in his neck and, as a result, he would not look up for too long.

After the longest time yet, longer than his wait at the gigantic hole and longer than his wait while he was out to sea, combined, he gave up for the third time and said, "Well, I guess that settles that, the sky is greater than God's Love." Dejected, he crawled back into the Explorer and was about to return to his back yard when he heard a loud screeching sound rip through the sky. He cautiously poked his head out of the box and peeked up in time to see a flock of Sea Gulls. They were whirling, swooping, flying upside down, and screeching as loud as they could.

Amazed, Alexander came out of the box and glanced across the sky. Clouds were rolling end over end, rainbows burst across the sky in spectacular colors, the stars, moon, and sun all flickered on and off as if they were experiencing a power shortage, and everything with wings suddenly filled the air. All that could be heard was the un-orchestrated sounds of flapping wings, birdcalls, and buzzing insects. Then, as if someone tripped over the plug, everything in the entire universe went black.

It was darker than Alexander had ever known it to be. Somewhere, off in the far distance, and after what seemed like eons, a low, dragging, droning sound could be heard. It sounded like a weak car battery that was trying desperately to start the car but it just didn't have the energy.
"Shhhrrrr, Shhrrrr, Shhrrrr."

After a while, the sun finally came back on. Alexander shielded his eyes from the bright light again and, once his eyes had adjusted, he could see something far, far away in the sky hurtling directly towards him. As it got closer, he realized that it was the arrow. Within seconds, even before Alexander could jump back, it penetrated the tiny plot of earth in between Alexander's feet.

The arrow entered the ground with a loud "THUD." The long line of twine was being sucked into the earth at a rapid speed. It sounded like someone sucking a spaghetti noodle into his or her mouth. At the end of the twine was the Love of God. Alexander bent down to pick it up and thought, "Wow, the only thing on top of the ground was the love." The arrow and all of the twine, except that part that was tied to the love, had disappeared somewhere deep into the bowels of the earth.

Alexander stooped down and untied the twine. When he did, the remaining portion of twine disappeared into the ground, as if the arrow were still moving. As he stood up, he could hear a voice that seemed to come from the very throat of the galaxy. It was the voice of the sky and it said, "I tried to hold the Love of God, but to hold such a Great Love *before* the time would cause me to break open and reveal the very Throne of God. Alas, I cannot contain this love. This love, God's Love, can only be held, consumed, and contained by the heart of man."

"My Lord," Alexander exclaimed, in his best southern drawl, mimicking his grandmother. He slipped the love back into his heart. It filled his heart up and wobbled and wiggled on the inside like a bowl of Jell-o. It felt warm and ticklish. Alexander grabbed his sides and giggled. He raced back to the Explorer and within no time at all, he was back in his backyard. Crawling out of the box, he came to his feet and took off in the direction of the house yelling, "Grandpa, Grandpa." Grandpa heard him calling and went to the back porch.

"Yes, Alexander, what is it?"

Out of breath, Alexander said, "You were right, Grandpa. The

Love of God is Great. It's greater than the earth, greater than the sea, and greater than the sky. It's the best-est love of all and it's inside of me! Thank you Grandpa for giving it to me." With that, Alexander leaped into Grandpa's arms and gave him a big hug and a kiss.

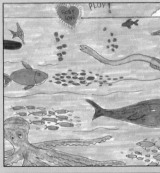
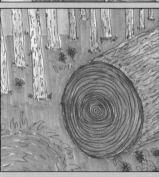

## The End

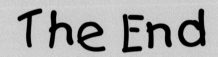

Printed in the United States
by Baker & Taylor Publisher Services